cops and robbers in which a house is built
the squirrel the hare and the little grey
days with frog and toad thomas the tank
le bear the three little w [barcode D1346521] the big
built at pooh corner for eeyore the story
grey rabbit my naughty little sister at the
tank engine the adventures of toad a kiss
big bad pig cops and robbers in which a
story of babar the squirrel the hare and
ter at the party days with frog and toad
toad a kiss for little bear the three little
s in which a house is built at pooh corner
the hare and the little grey rabbit my
frog and toad thomas the tank engine the
hree little wolves and the big bad pig cops
h corner for eeyore the story of babar the
my naughty little sister at the party days
the adventures of toad a kiss for little bear

The Childhood Collection

Ten Complete Picture Classics

HEINEMANN YOUNG BOOKS

CONTENTS

the three little wolves and the big bad

big · eugene trivizas · helen oxenbury

the three little wolves and the big bad

big · eugene trivizas · helen oxenbury

the three little wolves and the big bad

big · eugene trivizas · helen oxenbury

the three little wolves and the big bad

big · eugene trivizas · helen oxenbury

the three little wolves and the big bad

big · eugene trivizas · helen oxenbury

the three little wolves and the big bad

big · eugene trivizas · helen oxenbury

the three little wolves and the big bad

THE
THREE LITTLE WOLVES
AND THE
BIG BAD PIG

Eugene Trivizas

ILLUSTRATED BY

Helen Oxenbury

Once upon a time there were three cuddly little wolves with soft fur and fluffy tails who lived with their mother. The first was black, the second was grey and the third white.

One day the mother called the three little wolves round her and said, "My children, it is time for you to go out into the world. Go and build a house for yourselves. But beware of the big bad pig."

"Don't worry, Mother, we will watch out for him," said the three little wolves and they set off.

Soon they met a kangaroo who was pushing a
wheelbarrow full of red and yellow bricks.

"Please, will you give us some
of your bricks?" asked
the three little wolves.

"Certainly," said the kangaroo, and she gave them
lots of red and yellow bricks.

So the three little wolves built themselves a
house of bricks.

The very next day, the big bad pig came prowling
down the road and saw the house of bricks that
the little wolves had built.

   The three little wolves were playing croquet
in the garden. When they saw
the big bad pig coming,
they ran inside the house
and locked the door.

The pig knocked on the door and grunted,
  "Little wolves, little wolves, let me come in!"

"No, no, no," said the three little wolves. "By the hair on our chinny-chin-chins, we will not let you in, not for all the tea leaves in our china teapot!"

"Then I'll huff and I'll puff and I'll blow your house down!" said the pig.

So he huffed and he puffed and he puffed and he huffed, but the house didn't fall down.

But the pig wasn't called big and bad for nothing.
He went and fetched his sledgehammer and he
knocked the house down.

The three little wolves only just managed to escape before the bricks crumbled, and they were very frightened indeed.

"We shall have to build a stronger house," they said.
Just then, they saw a beaver who was mixing
concrete in a concrete mixer.

"Please, will you give us some of your concrete?"
asked the three little wolves.

"Certainly," said the beaver and he gave them buckets and buckets full of messy, slurry concrete.

So the three wolves built themselves a house of concrete.

No sooner had they finished than the big bad pig came prowling down the road and saw the house of concrete that the little wolves had built.

They were playing battledore and shuttlecock in the garden and when they saw the big bad pig coming, they ran inside their house and shut the door.

The pig rang the bell and said, "Little frightened wolves, let me come in!"

"No, no, no," said the three little wolves. "By the hair on our chinny-chin-chins, we will not let you in, not for all the tea leaves in our china teapot."

"Then I'll huff and I'll puff and I'll blow your house down!" said the pig.

So he huffed and he puffed and he puffed and he huffed, but the house didn't fall down.

But the pig wasn't called big and bad for nothing.
He went and fetched his pneumatic drill and
smashed the house down.

The three little wolves managed to escape but their chinny-chin-chins were trembling and trembling and trembling.

"We shall build an even stronger house," they said, because they were very determined. Just then, they saw a lorry coming along the road carrying barbed wire, iron bars, armour plates and heavy metal padlocks.

"Please, will you give us some of your barbed wire, a few iron bars and armour plates, and some heavy metal padlocks?" they said to the rhinoceros who was driving the lorry.

"Sure," said the rhinoceros and gave them plenty of barbed wire, iron bars, armour plates and heavy metal padlocks. He also gave them some plexiglass and some reinforced steel chains because he was a generous and kind-hearted rhinoceros.

So the three little wolves built themselves an extremely strong house. It was the strongest, securest house one could possibly imagine. They felt very relaxed and absolutely safe.

The next day, the big bad pig came prowling along
the road as usual. The little wolves were playing
hopscotch in the garden. When they saw the big bad
pig coming, they ran inside their house, bolted the
door and locked all the sixty-seven padlocks.

The pig pressed the video entrance phone and
said, "Frightened little wolves with the trembling
chins, let me come in!"

"No, no, no!" said the little wolves. "By the hair on our chinny-chin-chins, we will not let you in, not for all the tea leaves in our china teapot."

"Then I'll huff and I'll puff and I'll blow your house down!" said the pig.

So he huffed and he puffed and he puffed and he huffed, but the house didn't fall down.

But the pig wasn't called big and bad for nothing. He brought some dynamite, laid it against the house, lit the fuse and . . .

the house
blew up.

The little wolves
just managed to escape
with their fluffy tails scorched.

"Something must be wrong with our building materials," they said. "We have to try something different. But *what*?"

At that moment, they saw a flamingo bird coming along pushing a wheelbarrow full of flowers.

"Please, will you give us some flowers?" asked the little wolves.

"With pleasure," said the flamingo bird and gave them lots of flowers. So the three little wolves built themselves a house of flowers.

One wall was of marigolds, one wall of daffodils, one wall of pink roses and one wall of cherry blossom. The ceiling was made of sunflowers and the floor was a carpet of daisies. They had water lilies in their bathtub and buttercups in their fridge. It was a rather fragile house and it swayed in the wind, but it was very beautiful.

Next day, the big bad pig came prowling down the road and saw the house of flowers that the little wolves had built.

He rang the bluebell and said, "Little frightened wolves with the trembling chins and the scorched tails, let me come in!"

"No, no, no," said the three little wolves. "By the hair on our chinny-chin-chins, we will not let you in, not for all the tea leaves in our china teapot!"

"Then I'll huff and I'll puff and I'll blow your house down!" said the pig.

But as he took a deep breath, ready to huff and puff, he smelled the soft scent of the flowers. It was fantastic. And because the scent took his breath away, the pig took another breath and then another. Instead of huffing and puffing, he began to sniff.

He sniffed deeper and deeper until he was quite filled with the fragrant scent. His heart became tender and he realized how horrible he had been in the past. In other words, he became a big *good* pig. He started to sing and to dance the tarantella.

At first, the three little wolves were a bit worried, thinking that it might be a trick, but soon they realized that the pig had truly changed, so they came running out of the house. They introduced themselves and started playing games with him.

First they played pig-pog and then piggy-in-the-middle and when they were all tired, they invited him into the house.

They offered him china tea and strawberries
and wolfberries, and asked him to stay with
them as long as he wanted.
The pig accepted, and they all lived happily
together ever after.

cops and robbers · janet and allan
ahlberg · cops and robbers · janet and
allan ahlberg · cops and robbers
janet and allan ahlberg · cops and
robbers · janet and allan ahlberg · cops
and robbers · janet and allan ahlberg
cops and robbers · janet and allan
ahlberg · cops and robbers · janet and
allan ahlberg · cops and robbers · janet
and allan ahlberg · cops and robbers
janet and allan ahlberg · cops and
robbers · janet and allan ahlberg · cops
and robbers · janet and allan ahlberg
cops and robbers · janet and allan
ahlberg · cops and robbers · janet and

Cops
and
Robbers

Janet & Allan Ahlberg

Here are the cops of London town,
Hardworking, brave and true.
They drink their tea,
Stay up till three
And take good care of you.

Here are the robbers of London town
With crowbars and skeleton keys.
They prowl and creep
When you're asleep
And take . . . whatever they please.

Ho Ho for the robbers
The cops and the robbers Ho Ho!

The worst of the robbers,
          as most of us know,
Is dreadful Grabber Dan.
His voice is gruff
And he's pinched enough stuff
To fill a furniture van.

His mates in the gang are Snatcher Jack
And baby-faced Billy-the-Bag;
Peg-leg Horace,
Fingers Maurice
And villainous Grandma Swagg.

Ho Ho for the robbers
The cops and the robbers Ho Ho!

Grabber Dan

Snatcher Jack

Billy-the-Bag

Peg-leg Horace

Fingers Maurice

Grandma Swagg

This dreadful, snatching, pilfering bunch
Would rob a baby of his lunch.

This sneaking, creeping, fingering lot
Would burgle a burglar, like as not.

This peg-legged, baby-faced, villainous crew
Would pick the pocket of a kangaroo.

Now, we hear, there's worse to come,
For the robbers are planning –
              the scalliwag scum –
To make a haul on Christmas Eve
Of all the toys that they can thieve.
Like crooked santas they'll creep about,
Pinching presents – not giving them out.

Ho Ho for the robbers
The cops and the robbers Ho Ho!

The best of the cops, by common consent,
Is upstanding Officer Pugh.
He can run like a hare
And fight like a bear;
And he's good at crosswords too.

So on Christmas Eve when the trouble began
The station sergeant said,
"The thing to do
Is to send for Pugh,
He'll get 'em – alive or dead!"

"Listen Pugh," said the sergeant,
                    "the problem is this,
There are toys going missing galore.
From the size of the job,
We suspect it's a mob.
What they need's the strong arm of the Law!"

Ho Ho for the robbers
The cops and the robbers Ho Ho!

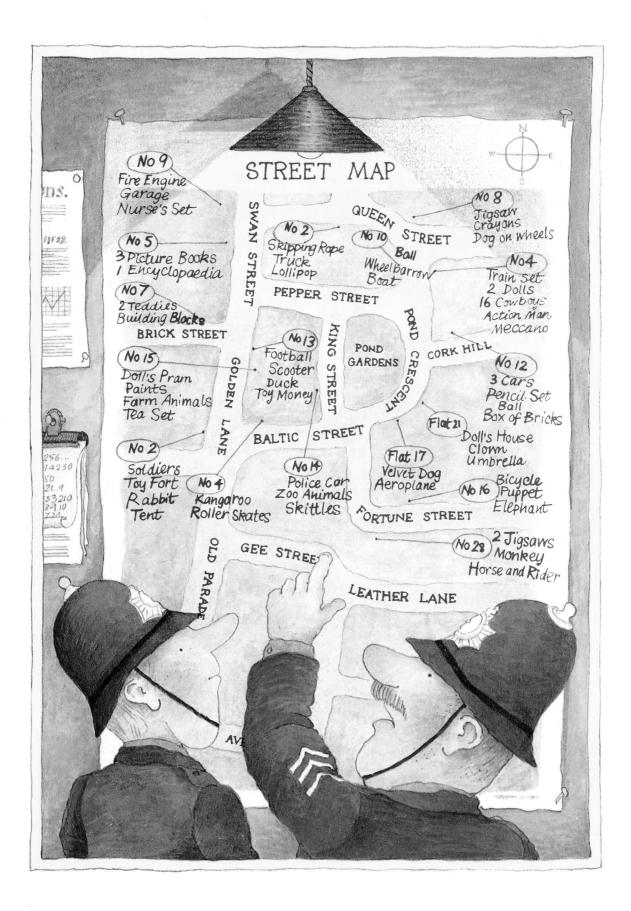

Meanwhile outside in the gloomy street
The strong arm of the robbers was working a treat,
And the strong leg too and the beady eye
Keeping watch for passers-by.
In at the windows, in at the doors,
Down the chimneys, under the floors,
Through silent rooms the robbers crept
While in their beds the children slept,

Dreaming of Santa Claus and snow
And what they'd get from Uncle Joe.
They never knew that "Uncle" Maurice
Was robbing them – and "Uncle" Horace.

Ho Ho for the robbers
The cops and the robbers Ho Ho!

The look-out man was Snatcher Jack;
He stood in a doorway yawning.
But when Officer Pugh
Came into view,
Jack saw him and whistled a warning.

Grandma Swagg, when the warning came,
Was pushing a pram up the road.
It was piled high with loot
And stolen to boot,
A thoroughly villainous load.

"Hallo, hallo," said Officer Pugh,
"Now then, what's going on here?"
"Not much, young man,"
Said the criminal gran,
"We're just having a robbery, dear."

Ho Ho for the robbers
The cops and the robbers Ho Ho!

Before Officer Pugh could unravel this clue
The robbers were on him like beasts from a zoo.

They knocked off his helmet and rumpled his tie,
Trod on his truncheon, kicked mud in his eye,

Pulled his ears and tickled his feet,
Threw half of his clothes all over the street,

Punched and pummelled him – Wham – Bam – SLAM
Even ran over him with the pram.

"Give up, give up!" the robbers cried
As they sat on the officer side by side.
"We've got you out-numbered five to one."
(For in the confusion, Grandma had gone.)
But Officer Pugh just shook his head.
"We've hardly started, boys," he said,
And he laughed a laugh and grinned a grin.
"Sitting comfortably are you? Then I'll begin!"

With a sudden leap he bounded free
And handcuffed Horace to a nearby tree;

Tied Maurice up in an empty sack
And beat the daylights out of Jack.

"Help!" shouted Billy. "This can't be fair;
That Pugh's not human – he fights like a bear.
My mother was right – crime doesn't pay!"
And with these words he fainted away.

Grabber Dan was the last to cop it
(Grandma, of course, having chosen to hop it).
Dan tried to hide – the officer sought him.
Dan tried to run – the officer caught him.
Dan went to lift Pugh over his head.
The officer lifted Dan instead,
And whirled him round and swung him – WHOOSH!
Across the road and into a bush.

Down he tumbled, skidded, rolled;
Hit a concrete gnome and was knocked out cold.
Pugh dusted his hands and sat on the wall.
A little snow had begun to fall.
He looked at the gnome and patted its head.
"You could get a medal for this," he said.

Ho Ho for the robbers
The cops and the robbers Ho Ho!

Here are the cops of London town
In the station at half-past two.
They drink their beer
And raise a cheer
For upstanding Officer Pugh.

Here are the robbers of London town
In cells all gloomy and grim.
"Let us out, let us out!
Not guilty!" they shout,
And, "It wasn't me – it was him!"

Ho Ho for the robbers
The cops and the robbers Ho Ho!

And the toys? Oh, they were taken back
By a Santa Claus copper with a Santa Claus sack.
While the rest of the force searched day and night
For an elderly lady of medium height
With a fondness for earrings and red fox furs
And a habit of taking what wasn't hers.
She usually carried a sizeable bag;
Her name, of course, was Grandma Swagg.

Ho Ho for the robbers
The cops and the robbers Ho Ho!

in which a house is built at pooh corner for eeyore · a a milne · e h shepard

In Which a House is Built at Pooh Corner for Eeyore

*A A Milne
and
E H Shepard*

One day when Pooh Bear had nothing else to do, he thought he would do something, so he went round to Piglet's house to see what Piglet was doing. It was still snowing as he stumped over the white forest track, and he expected to find Piglet warming his toes in front of his fire, but to his surprise he saw that the door was open, and the more he looked inside the more Piglet wasn't there.

"He's out," said Pooh sadly. "That's what it is. He's not in. I shall have to go on a fast Thinking Walk by myself. Bother!"

But first he thought that he would knock very loudly just to make *quite* sure . . . and while he waited for Piglet not to answer, he jumped up and down to keep warm, and a hum came suddenly into his head, which seemed to him a Good Hum, such as is Hummed Hopefully to Others.

> The more it snows
> (Tiddely pom),
> The more it goes
> (Tiddely pom),
> The more it goes
> (Tiddely pom),
> On Snowing.
> And nobody knows
> (Tiddely pom),
> How cold my toes
> (Tiddely pom),
> How cold my toes
> (Tiddely pom),
> Are growing.

"So what I'll do," said Pooh, "is I'll do this. I'll just go home first and see what the time is, and perhaps I'll put a muffler round my neck, and then I'll go and see Eeyore and sing it to him."

He hurried back to his own house; and his mind was so busy on the way with the hum that he was getting ready for Eeyore that, when he suddenly saw Piglet sitting in his best arm-chair, he could only stand there rubbing his head and wondering whose house he was in.

"Hallo, Piglet," he said. "I thought you were out."

"No," said Piglet, "it's you who were out, Pooh."

"So it was," said Pooh. "I knew one of us was."

He looked up at his clock, which had stopped at five minutes to eleven some weeks ago.

"Nearly eleven o'clock," said Pooh happily. "You're just in time for a little smackerel of something," and he put his head into the cupboard. "And then we'll go out, Piglet, and sing my song to Eeyore."

"Which song, Pooh?"

"The one we're going to sing to Eeyore," explained Pooh.

The clock was still saying five minutes to eleven when Pooh and Piglet set out on their way half an hour later. The wind had dropped, and the snow, tired of rushing round in circles trying to catch itself up, now fluttered gently down until it found a place on which to rest, and sometimes the place was Pooh's nose and sometimes it wasn't and in a little while Piglet was wearing a white muffler round his neck and feeling more snowy behind the ears than he had ever felt before.

"Pooh," he said at last, and a little timidly, because he didn't want Pooh to think he was Giving In, "I was just wondering. How would it be if we went home now and *practised* your song, and then sang it to Eeyore tomorrow – or – or the next day, when we happen to see him?"

"That's a very good idea, Piglet," said Pooh. "We'll practise it now as we go along. But it's no good going home to practise it, because it's a special Outdoor Song which Has To Be Sung In The Snow."

"Are you sure?" asked Piglet anxiously.

"Well, you'll see, Piglet, when you listen. Because this is how it begins. *The more it snows, tiddely pom—*"

"Tiddely what?" said Piglet.

"Pom," said Pooh. "I put that in to make it more hummy. *The more it goes, tiddely pom, the more—*"

"Didn't you say snows?"

"Yes, but that was *before*."

"Before the tiddely pom?"

"It was a *different* tiddely pom," said Pooh, feeling rather muddled now. "I'll sing it to you properly and then you'll see."

So he sang it again.

The more it
SNOWS-tiddely-pom,
The more it
GOES-tiddely-pom
The more it
GOES-tiddely-pom
On
Snowing.

And nobody
KNOWS-tiddely-pom,
How cold my
TOES-tiddely-pom
How cold my
TOES-tiddely-pom
Are
Growing.

He sang it like that, which is much the best way of singing it, and when he had finished, he waited for Piglet to say that, of all the Outdoor Hums for Snowy Weather he had ever heard, this was the best. And, after thinking the matter out carefully, Piglet said:

"Pooh," he said solemnly, "it isn't the *toes* so much as the *ears*."

By this time they were getting near Eeyore's Gloomy Place, which was where he lived, and as it was still very snowy behind Piglet's ears, and he was getting tired of it, they turned into a little pine-wood, and sat down on the gate which led into it. They were out of the snow now, but it was very cold, and to keep themselves warm they sang Pooh's song right through six times, Piglet doing the tiddely-poms and Pooh doing the rest of it, and both of them thumping on the top of the gate with pieces of stick at the proper places. And in a little while they felt much warmer, and were able to talk again.

"I've been thinking," said Pooh, "and what I've been thinking is this. I've been thinking about Eeyore."

"What about Eeyore?"

"Well, poor Eeyore has nowhere to live."

"Nor he has," said Piglet.

"*You* have a house, Piglet, and I have a house, and they are very good houses. And Christopher Robin has a house, and Owl and Kanga and Rabbit have houses, and even Rabbit's friends and relations have houses or somethings, but poor Eeyore has nothing. So what I've been thinking is: Let's build him a house."

"That," said Piglet, "is a Grand Idea. Where shall we build it?"

"We will build it here," said Pooh, "just by this wood, out of the wind, because this is where I thought of it. And we will call this Pooh Corner. And we will build an Eeyore House with sticks at Pooh Corner for Eeyore."

"There was a heap of sticks on the other side of the wood," said Piglet. "I saw them. Lots and lots. All piled up."

"Thank you, Piglet," said Pooh. "What you have just said will be a Great Help to us, and because of it I could call this place Poohanpiglet Corner if Pooh Corner didn't sound better, which it does, being smaller and more like a corner. Come along."

So they got down off the gate and went round to the other side of the wood to fetch the sticks.

Christopher Robin had spent the morning indoors going to Africa and back, and he had just got off the boat and was wondering what it was like outside, when who should come knocking at the door but Eeyore.

"Hallo, Eeyore," said Christopher Robin, as he opened the door and came out. "How are *you*?"

"It's snowing still," said Eeyore gloomily.

"So it is."

"*And* freezing."

"Is it?"

"Yes," said Eeyore. "However," he said, brightening up a little, "we haven't had an earthquake lately."

"What's the matter, Eeyore?"

"Nothing, Christopher Robin. Nothing important. I suppose you haven't seen a house or what-not anywhere about?"

"What sort of a house?"

"Just a house."

"Who lives there?"

"I do. At least I thought I did. But I suppose I don't. After all, we can't all have houses."

"But, Eeyore, I didn't know – I always thought—"

"I don't know how it is, Christopher Robin, but what with all this snow and one thing and another, not to mention icicles and such-like, it isn't so Hot in my field about three o'clock in the morning as some people think it is. It isn't Close, if you know what I mean - not so as to be uncomfortable. It isn't Stuffy. In fact, Christopher Robin," he went on in a loud whisper, "quite-between-ourselves-and-don't-tell-anybody, it's Cold."

"Oh, Eeyore!"

"And I said to myself: The others will be sorry if I'm getting myself all cold. They haven't got Brains, any of them, only grey fluff that's blown into their heads by mistake, and they don't Think, but if it goes on snowing for another six weeks or so, one of them will begin to say to himself: 'Eeyore can't be so very much too Hot about three o'clock in the morning.' And then it will Get About. And they'll be Sorry."

"Oh, Eeyore!" said Christopher Robin, feeling very sorry already.

"I don't mean you, Christopher Robin. You're different. So what it all comes to is that I built myself a house down by my little wood."

"Did you really? How exciting!"

"The really exciting part," said Eeyore in his most melancholy voice, "is that when I left it this morning it was there, and when I came back it wasn't. Not at all, very natural, and it was only Eeyore's house. But still I just wondered."

Christopher Robin didn't stop to wonder. He was already back in *his* house, putting on his waterproof hat, his waterproof boots, and his waterproof macintosh as fast as he could.

"We'll go and look for it at once," he called out to Eeyore.

"Sometimes," said Eeyore, "when people have quite finished taking a person's house, there are one or two bits which they don't want and are rather glad for the person to take back, if you know what I mean. So I thought if we just went—"

"Come on," said Christopher Robin, and off they hurried, and in a very little time they got to the corner of the field by the side of the pine-wood, where Eeyore's house wasn't any longer.

"There!" said Eeyore. "Not a stick of it left! Of course, I've still got all this snow to do what I like with. One mustn't complain."

But Christopher Robin wasn't listening to Eeyore, he was listening to something else.

"Can you hear it?" he asked.

"What is it? Somebody laughing?"

"Listen."

They both listened . . . and they heard a deep gruff voice saying in a singing voice that the more it snowed the more it went on snowing, and a small high voice tiddely-pomming in between.

"It's Pooh," said Christopher Robin excitedly. . . .

"Possibly," said Eeyore.

"*And* Piglet!" said Christopher Robin excitedly.

"Probably," said Eeyore. "What we *want* is a Trained Bloodhound."

The words of the song changed suddenly.

"*We've finished our HOUSE!*" sang the gruff voice.

"*Tiddely pom!*" sang the squeaky one.

"*It's a beautiful HOUSE . . .*"
"*Tiddely pom . . .*"
"*I wish it were MINE . . .*"
"*Tiddely pom . . .*"
"Pooh!" shouted Christopher Robin. . . .
The singers on the gate stopped suddenly.
"It's Christopher Robin!" said Pooh eagerly.
"He's round by the place where we got all those sticks from," said Piglet.
"Come on," said Pooh.

They climbed down their gate and hurried round the corner of the wood, Pooh making welcoming noises all the way.

"Why, here *is* Eeyore," said Pooh, when he had finished hugging Christopher Robin, and he nudged Piglet, and Piglet nudged him, and they thought to themselves what a lovely surprise they had got ready. "Hallo, Eeyore."

"Same to you, Pooh Bear, and twice on Thursdays," said Eeyore gloomily.

Before Pooh could say: "Why Thursdays?" Christopher Robin began to explain the sad story of Eeyore's Lost House. And Pooh and Piglet listened, and their eyes seemed to get bigger and bigger.

"*Where* did you say it was?" asked Pooh.

"Just here," said Eeyore.

"Made of sticks?"

"Yes."

"Oh!" said Piglet.

"What?" said Eeyore.

"I just said 'Oh!'" said Piglet nervously. And so as to seem quite at ease he hummed tiddely-pom once or twice in a what-shall-we-do-now kind of way.

"You're sure it *was* a house?" said Pooh. "I mean, you're sure the house was just here?"

"Of course I am," said Eeyore. And he murmured to himself, "No brain at all, some of them."

"Why, what's the matter, Pooh?" asked Christopher Robin.

"Well," said Pooh . . . "The fact *is*," said Pooh . . . "Well, the fact *is*," said Pooh . . . "You see," said Pooh . . . "It's like this," said Pooh, and something seemed to tell him that he wasn't explaining very well, and he nudged Piglet again.

"It's like this," said Piglet quickly. . . . "Only warmer," he added after deep thought.

"What's warmer?"

"The other side of the wood, where Eeyore's house is."

"*My* house?" said Eeyore. "My house was here."

"No," said Piglet firmly. "The other side of the wood."

"Because of being warmer," said Pooh.

"But I ought to *know*—"

"Come and look," said Piglet simply, and he led the way.

"There wouldn't be *two* houses," said Pooh. "Not so close together."

They came round the corner, and there was Eeyore's house, looking as comfy as anything.

"There you are," said Piglet.

"Inside as well as outside," said Pooh proudly.

Eeyore went inside . . . and came out again.

"It's a remarkable thing," he said. "It *is* my house, and I built it where I said I did, so the wind must have blown it here. And the wind blew it right over the wood, and blew it down here, and here it is as good as ever. In fact, better in places."

"Much better," said Pooh and Piglet together.

"It just shows what can be done by taking a little trouble," said Eeyore. "Do you see, Pooh? Do you see, Piglet? Brains first and then Hard Work. Look at it! *That's* the way to build a house," said Eeyore proudly.

So they left him in it; and Christopher Robin went back to lunch with his friends Pooh and Piglet, and on the way they told him of the Awful Mistake they had made. And when he had finished laughing, they all sang the Outdoor Song for Snowy Weather the rest of the way home, Piglet, who was still not quite sure of his voice, putting in the tiddely-poms again.

"And I know it *seems* easy," said Piglet to himself, "but it isn't *every one* who could do it."

THE STORY OF BABAR

THE LITTLE ELEPHANT

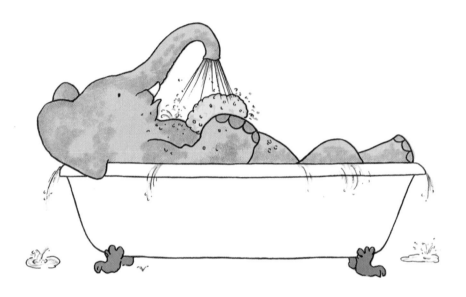

Jean de Brunhoff

In the Great Forest
a little elephant was born.
His name was Babar.
His mother loved him dearly,
and used to rock him to sleep
with her trunk,
singing to him softly the while.

Babar grew fast. Soon he was playing
with the other baby elephants.

He was one of the nicest of them.
Look at him digging in the sand with a shell.

One day Babar was having a lovely ride
on his mother's back,
when a cruel hunter,
hiding behind a bush,
shot at them.

He killed Babar's mother.
The monkey hid himself, the birds flew away,
and Babar burst into tears.
The hunter ran up
to catch poor Babar.

Babar was very frightened
and ran away
from the hunter.
After some days,
tired and footsore,
he came to a town.

He was amazed,
for it was
the first time
he had ever seen
so many houses.

What strange things he saw!
Beautiful avenues!
Motorcars and motorbuses!
But what interested Babar
most of all was
two gentlemen
he met in the street.

He thought to himself:
"What lovely clothes they have got!
I wish I could
have some too!
But how can I get them?"

Luckily, he was seen by
a very rich old lady
who understood
little elephants,
and knew at once
that he was longing for
a smart suit.
She loved making others happy,
so she gave him
her purse.

"Thank you, Madam,"
said Babar.

Without wasting a moment
Babar went into a big shop.
He got into the lift.
It was such fun going up and down
in this jolly little box,
that he went ten times to the very top
and ten times down again to the bottom.

He was going up once more
when the lift-boy said to him:
"Sir, this is not a toy.
You must get out now
and buy what you want.
Look, here is
the shop-walker."

Then he bought

a shirt,
collar
and
tie,

a suit
of a
delightful
green
colour,

next
a lovely
bowler
hat,

and
finally
shoes
and
spats.

Babar was so pleased
with his purchases,
and satisfied
with his appearance
that he paid a visit
to the photographer.

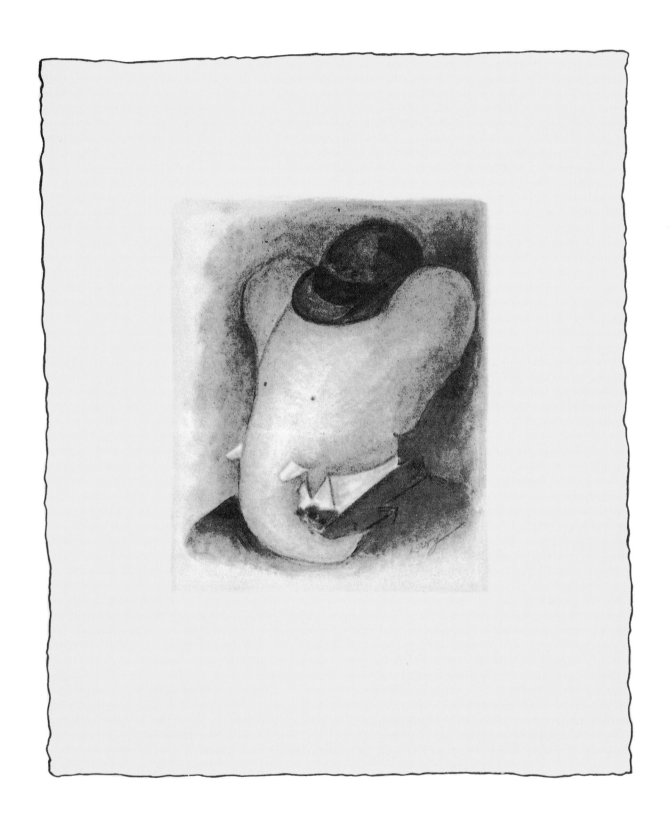

And here is his photograph.

Babar went to dinner
with his friend the old lady.
She, too, thought he looked very smart
in his new suit.
After dinner, he was so tired,
that he went early to sleep.

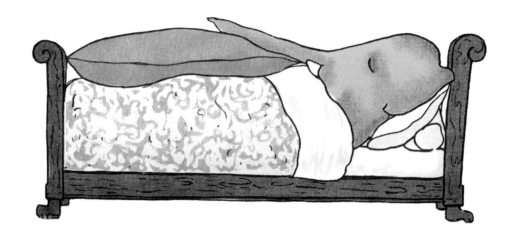

Babar made his home
in the old lady's house.
Every morning
they did their exercises together,
and then Babar had
his bath.

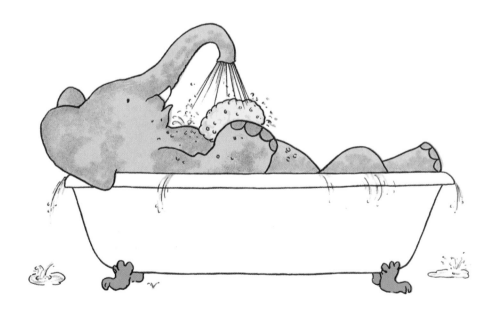

Every day he drove out in the car
that the old lady had bought him.
She gave him everything that he wanted.

A learned professor gave him lessons.
Babar was attentive,
and always gave the right answer.
He was a most promising pupil.

In the evenings, after dinner,
he told the old lady's friends
all about his life in the Great Forest.

And yet
Babar was not altogether happy:
he could no longer play about
in the Great Forest
with his little cousins
and his friends the monkeys.
He often gazed
out of the window
dreaming of his childhood,
and when he thought of
his dear mother
he used to cry.

Two years passed by.
One day he was out for a walk,
when he met two little elephants
with no clothes on.
"Why, here are Arthur and Celeste,
my two little cousins!"
he cried in amazement to the old lady.

Babar hugged Arthur and Celeste
and took them to buy some lovely clothes.

Next, he took them to a tea-shop,
where they had some delicious cakes.

Meanwhile in the Great
Forest all the elephants
were searching for Arthur
and Celeste and
their mothers

grew more and more anxious.
Luckily, an old bird flying over
the town had spied them, and
hurried back to tell
the elephants.

The mothers went to the town
to fetch Arthur and Celeste.
They were very glad when they found them,
but they scolded them all the same
for having run away.

Babar made up his mind
to return to the Great Forest
with Arthur and Celeste and their mothers.
The old lady
helped him to pack.

When everything was ready for the journey
Babar kissed his old friend good-bye.
If he had not been so sorry to leave her
he would have been delighted to go home.
He promised to come back to her,
and never to forget her.

Off they went!
There was no room
for the mother elephants
in the car.
So they ran behind,
lifting their trunks
so as not to breathe in
the dust.
The old lady
was left alone,
sadly thinking:
"When shall I see my little Babar again?"

Alas! That very day the King of the elephants
had eaten a bad mushroom.

It had poisoned him. He had been very ill,
and then had died.
It was a terrible misfortune.

After his funeral
the oldest elephants met together
to choose a new King.

Just at that moment they heard
a noise and turned round.
What a wonderful sight they saw!
It was Babar arriving in his car,
with all the elephants running and shouting:
"Here they are! Here they are!
They have come back!
Hullo, Babar! Hullo, Arthur!
Hullo, Celeste!
What lovely clothes!
What a beautiful car!"

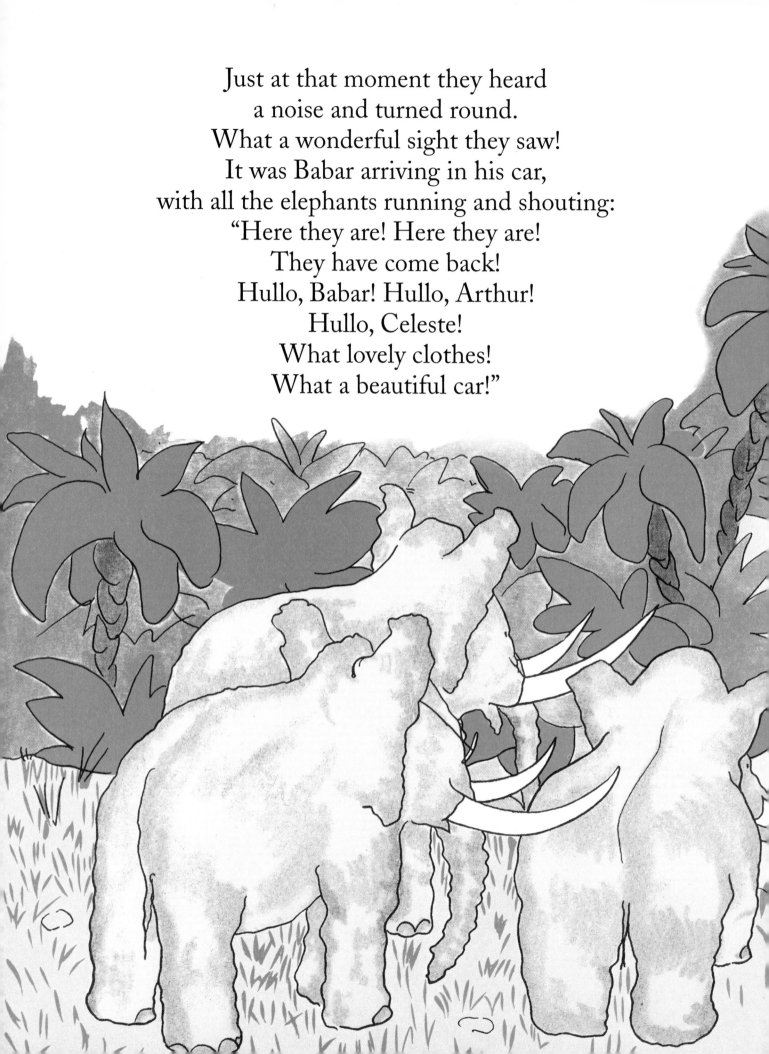

Then Cornelius,
the oldest elephant of all,
said, in his quavering voice:
"My dear friends, we must have a new King.
Why not choose Babar?
He has come back from the town,
where he has lived among men and learnt much.
Let us offer him the crown."

All the elephants thought
that Cornelius had spoken wisely,
and they listened eagerly
to hear what Babar would say.

"I thank you all,"
said Babar;
"but before accepting the crown
I must tell you
that on our journey in the car
Celeste and I
got engaged to be married.
If I become your King, she will be your Queen."

Long live Queen Celeste!
Long live King Babar!!

the elephants shouted with one voice.
And that was how Babar became King.

"Cornelius," said Babar,
"you have such good ideas
that I shall make you a general,
and when I get my crown
I will give you my hat.
In a week's time
I am going to marry Celeste.
We will give a grand party
to celebrate our marriage
and our coronation."
And Babar asked the birds
to take invitations to all the animals,

and he told the dromedary to go to the town
to buy him some fine wedding clothes.

The guests began to arrive.
The dromedary brought the clothes
just in time for the ceremony.

After the wedding and the coronation

everyone danced merrily.

The Party was over.
Night fell,
and the stars came out.
The hearts of
King Babar and Queen Celeste
were filled with
happy dreams.

Then all the world slept.
The guests had gone home,
very pleased and very tired
after dancing so much.
For many a long day
they will remember
that wonderful ball.

Then King Babar and Queen Celeste
set out on their honeymoon,
in a glorious yellow balloon,
to meet with new adventures.

The Squirrel, the Hare
and the
Little Grey Rabbit

Alison Uttley

Pictures by
Margaret Tempest

Along time ago there lived in a little house on the edge of a wood, a Hare, a Squirrel, and a little Grey Rabbit.

The Hare, who wore a blue coat on weekdays and a red coat on Sundays, was a conceited fellow.

The Squirrel, who wore a brown dress on weekdays, and a yellow dress on Sundays, was proud.

But the little Rabbit, who always wore a grey dress with white collar and cuffs, was not proud at all.

Every morning when the birds began to twitter she sprang out of her bed in the attic and ran downstairs to the kitchen. She went into the shed for firewood, and lighted the fire. Then she filled her kettle with clear water from the brook which ran past the door, just beyond the garden.

While the water boiled she swept the floor and dusted the kitchen. She put the three small chairs round the table and spread a blue and white cloth. She made the tea in a brown teapot from daisy-heads which she kept in a canister on the dresser, and then she called the Squirrel and the Hare.

"Squirrel, wake up! Hare, Hare, breakfast is ready."

Downstairs they strolled, rubbing their eyes, and wriggling their ears, but the little Grey Rabbit was already in the garden, gathering lettuce.

"Good morning, Grey Rabbit," yawned the Hare. "I declare you have given us lettuce again. Really, my dear, you must think of something new for breakfast."

"Good morning, Grey Rabbit," said the Squirrel. "Where's the milk?"

"It hasn't come yet," she said.

"Tut," exclaimed the Squirrel. "Late again. We must get another milkman."

Just then "Tap, tap, tap" sounded on the door.

Little Grey Rabbit ran to open it and there stood the Hedgehog with a pint of milk.

"I nearly didn't get here at all," said he. "Such a dreadful thing has happened! A Weasel has come to live in the wood. They say it isn't safe to be out after dusk."

"Oh dear!" murmured the Grey Rabbit. "You must take care of yourself, even if we *do* go without milk."

"Bless your heart, my pretty dear," he smiled. "You shall have your milk as long as old Hedgehog has some prickles left."

"Well, good-day," he continued, "and take care of yourself, and warn those two grumblers within there," and off he hobbled.

"Whatever have you been talking about all this time?" asked the Squirrel angrily.

"Why was the milkman so late?" demanded the Hare.

Little Grey Rabbit drew her chair close up to them. "He says a Weasel has come to live in the wood nearby."

"A Weasel, child?" said the Squirrel. "Pooh! Who's afraid of a Weasel?"

But she shut the window and poked the fire, and kept the poker in her hand whilst she drank her milk.

"Tap, tap, tap," came on the door.

"Who's that?" asked the Squirrel.

Grey Rabbit opened the door a crack.

"It's only Robin Redbreast with the letters," cried she. "Come in, Robin, you quite startled us. Have you heard the news?"

"About the Weasel? Yes. He's a great big fellow with very sharp teeth. *I* shouldn't like to meet him on a dark night. Well, I must be off, I have to warn the birds," and away he flew.

All day the Hare and the Squirrel stayed in the kitchen. The little Grey Rabbit ran upstairs and made the beds. She swept the floors, dusted and tidied up after the other two. Then she got her basket and started out to do the marketing.

"You might get me a new teazle brush," called the Squirrel. "I must give my tail a good brush, it is quite tangled."

"And get me some young carrots," shouted the Hare. "I am tired of lettuce for breakfast."

Off ran the little Grey Rabbit, in her clean white collar and cuffs, and her basket on her arm. Over the brook she leapt, and then she went into the wood. She kept a very sharp look-out, and ran so softly that the leaves underfoot scarcely moved, and the grass hardly felt her weight. Once she heard a rustle behind her, but she went steadily on and dare not turn her head. Her heart went pitter-pat so loudly she thought it would burst, but it was only a blackbird in the beech leaves.

When she was through the wood she stopped a few minutes to rest and nibble some sweet, short grass. She found the teazle bushes growing in the hedge, among some nettles, and she bit off three prickly heads and put them in her basket.

Then, with a laugh of delight, she ran on till she got to the Farmer's garden. She passed the hole in the wall, for the gate was open, so in she tripped, over the lettuce and under the rhubarb to the carrot bed.

"I wish we could grow carrots at home," she said, as she pulled them up one by one and placed them carefully in her basket.

Swish! Swish! A sack was thrown over her and someone hit wildly at her with a rake.

Little Grey Rabbit ran this way and that, in the dark,

holding her breath, as she tried to dodge the blows. One hit the basket and nearly broke it, and hurt her paw, but still she ran. Then she found a gap, and out she darted, dodging in and out of the cabbage leaves, with the Farmer running after, close to her heels.

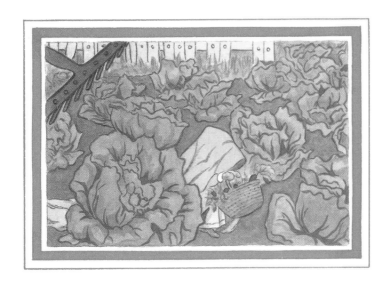

"You little rascal," he called, "you've been after my carrots. Just wait till I catch you." But Little Grey Rabbit did not wait. She could not stop to explain that she thought they were everybody's carrots.

No, she ran for her life, across the field, to the wood.

"I don't think I shall go there again," she said, as she licked her hurt paw, and put a dock-leaf bandage over it. "We must grow our own carrots. I will ask Wise Owl how to do it."

She hurried through the wood as softly as she had come, and reached home safely.

"What a long time you have been," grumbled the Hare. "Did you get my carrots?"

Little Grey Rabbit cooked the dinner, gathered the firewood, and then sat down to dry some herbs and prepare for the next day. She was such a busy little Rabbit she was never still a moment, but the Hare and the Squirrel sat one on each side of the fire and never moved except to put fresh wood on the blaze.

Night fell and they all went to bed, after locking and bolting the door and fastening the shutters. But when the moon shone in and the stars were twinkling, the little Grey Rabbit crept downstairs and opened the door. The moon was big in the sky and the stars winked and smiled at her. She stepped out on to the dewy grass, and closed the door softly.

Everywhere was silver white. Leaves and grass sparkled and a thousand sweet scents rose to her little twitching nostrils. How delicious it was!

Although she felt afraid of the Weasel, lurking like a wolf in the wood, she could not help turning head over heels and standing on her head for joy. She felt so young and free!

She jumped the brook three times in her excitement, and then trotted off to the wood. Her feet left a trail of footprints in the grass, so she turned round and walked backwards. Hopping and skipping and turning her head, twisting and twining in and out of the trees she went, with no adventure except a collision with a Pheasant, who rose screaming with fright.

At last she reached the Wise Owl's house, a hollow oak tree. He sat on a bough with shining eyes searching the wood, waiting to start out on his hunt for food.

Little Grey Rabbit quickly waved a white handkerchief for a truce, and he nodded down at her.

"Wise Owl," she began, "will you tell me how to grow carrots like those in the Farmer's garden?"

"What will you give me?" asked the Wise Owl, in a high, crying voice.

"Oh, dear, I haven't anything," she faltered, looking very sad.

"Yes you have," cried the Owl. "You can give me your tail."

"My tail?" she exclaimed in horror.

"Yes, your tail, or I shall not help you."

"You can have it," she cried bravely, "but be quick."

The Wise Owl hopped down and with one bite of his strong beak he cut it off and wrapped a cobweb round the stump. Then he fastened it on his front door as a door-knocker.

"You can grow carrots," said he solemnly, "with carrot seed."

"Where can I get it?" asked the Grey Rabbit.

"From the shop in the village."

And Wise Owl flapped his wings and flew away.

The little Grey Rabbit started home again. She stepped into her own footprints, but now and then a shiny round tear fell on the grass, and she gave a sigh.

Suddenly, as she turned a corner, she saw the Weasel standing in her path. His back was turned, he was examining the footprints.

"Ah!" cried he, "a Rabbit has gone this way," and he ran along in front of her. Little Grey Rabbit's heart banged and thumped as she followed a long way behind. When he came to the brook he was puzzled, and Grey Rabbit watched. At this side of the water the footprints went to the water's edge, but at the other side, too, they went towards the edge. He scratched his whiskers.

"She must have tumbled in and been drowned," said he, and he went off down the stream, hunting and sniffing.

Grey Rabbit leapt over, ran to the house, upstairs and into bed, where she slept and slept till the birds began to sing.

"That Weasel has been round the house in the night," said the Hedgehog as he delivered the milk the next morning.

"Whatever have you done with your tail?" said the Hare, staring at her as she bustled about getting breakfast.

"Grey Rabbit, where *is* your tail?" echoed the Squirrel, frowning at her.

"I gave it to Wise Owl," said Grey Rabbit, blushing and hanging her head.

"Disgraceful," said the Hare.

"Disgracefuller," said the Squirrel, not to be outdone.

A big tear ran down into her tea, and splashed her cuffs. She felt very unhappy, and wished Wise Owl would give her back her tail.

After dinner that day she took her basket and started off on her journey, leaving the two sitting dozing one on each side of the fire. They did not see her go, neither did they see the window open stealthily, and a black nose appear.

Little Grey Rabbit turned in another direction, and did not cross the brook. She went down the lane, overhung with honeysuckle and blackberry bushes.

When she came to the village it was very quiet, for the children were in school and the labourers had gone back to work in the fields. Dogs lay asleep on door-steps, and cats basked in the sun.

No one saw a little Grey Rabbit with a little grey shadow slip down the road, hesitate a moment outside the village shop, and then run through the open door.

She gazed about her with wide-open eyes. Wonderful things lay all about. Buckets and frying-pans, pots and cheeses, mouse-traps and cherry brandy. She was bewildered as she looked for the seeds.

Would she ever find them? Then she saw the picture of a carrot on a little packet, lying with other packets. Success at last! Here were lettuces and radishes, parsley, and cabbages.

Quickly she seized one of each kind. Then she saw a bag with a yellow bird on it, labelled "Canary Seed", so she took that too.

"I will plant that seed and have some little yellow birds as well as carrots in the garden," she thought.

The bag was heavy, and as she dragged it into the basket she made a noise.

Grey Rabbit picked up the basket and fled for the door.

She ran down the street as if an army were after her, but all was still, and, except for five ducks waddling across the road, she saw no one.

The journey home was pleasant, and she made plans as she tripped along in and out of the shadows.

"I shall dig up that bit of grass under the hedge and pick out the stones. Then I shall sow three rows of carrot seeds. I shall sow radishes next to them, and parsley next. I will dig that good piece in the middle for the bird seed, and when the young yellows come out they will make nests in the hedge."

"Ah," she went on, getting more and more delighted with her plans, "I may get hundreds and hundreds of little birds from this bag of seed, and hundreds of carrots from this packet, and hundreds of radishes from this, and hundreds – Goodness me, whatever is this?"

For she had reached home and the door stood wide open. No one was within. Upstairs she ran, in the bedrooms, in the attic and the box-room. No one was there. In the kitchen the chairs were upset and the table pushed on one side. Bits of red hair from Squirrel's tail lay on the floor, and the sleeve of Hare's coat lay dirty in a corner.

"Oh, my dear Squirrel, my darling Hare," she cried, with tears running down her cheeks. "Has that bad Weasel got you?"

She took a pair of scissors, a rope, and a stick, and started out to look for her companions.

Over the brook she found the trace of the Weasel, and at one side the grass was flattened and flowers were broken as if a heavy object had been dragged along.

"He has put them in a bag and dragged them home," she murmured, as she examined the track. "Poor, poor things! I do hope they are alive. If only I hadn't stopped so long choosing bird seed."

She hurried along the path, which took her through dark and gloomy glades, and brought her to an ugly black house, with the shutters up and nettles and weeds growing in the garden.

Then she lay down under a bush and waited.

A thick black smoke came out of the chimney, and she could hear the crackle of sticks. The door opened and a great savage Weasel stood on the doorstep.

"I shall need some more sticks after all," he said. "They will be safe in there."

He shut the door and turned the key in the lock. Then he ran about among the bushes picking up sticks.

"Too-whit, Too-whoo," called an Owl overhead. The Weasel looked up. He was afraid of Wise Owl, and he dared not move. The Owl saw Grey Rabbit, and knew her as the owner of his door-knocker.

But Grey Rabbit made a dash, seized the key, and was in the house whilst the Weasel still gazed up at the foe overhead. Then the Owl flew away, and he wiped his brow.

"That was a near thing," said he. "Now what about some acorn sauce?" And he stopped to pick up a few acorns and carried them in with his wood.

Little Grey Rabbit called, "Hare, Squirrel, where are you? It's me, it's Rabbit."

"Here, here; O, save us, dear Grey Rabbit," cried two piteous voices from a bag under the sofa.

Quickly Rabbit cut it open and let the two unhappy ones out, but they were so bruised and weak they could hardly walk.

"Upstairs with you," cried Grey Rabbit as the Weasel came home. "Take this rope and let yourselves out by the window. I will follow."

Then she seized a stool which stood on the hearth, and crept into the bag.

Grey Rabbit squeaked and moaned, and the Weasel chuckled as he piled the wood on the fire. Grey Rabbit lay watching him through the hole and waiting for a chance.

Upstairs Squirrel and Hare fastened the rope to a bed-post and slid down into the nettles. Away they went, struggling through the bushes, over brambles and across ditches.

Weasel opened the oven door. "I'll roast them both together," he said, putting some dripping in the tin. He took a stick and came to the bag. He dragged it out, and raised the stick, and, Bang! Down it came. Grey Rabbit crept inside the stool and lay protected by its legs. Bang! he went on the stool legs, but there was never a sound.

"Dead, both dead," said the Weasel. "Now is the oven ready?"

He opened the door and took hold of the hot tin. Quickly Grey Rabbit slipped out, gave him a great push into the tin and shut the oven door.

Off she ran, not stopping to hear his cries, but running as if he were after her. She never stopped till she got home, and as she sat panting in an arm-chair, the other two limped in.

"Oh, Grey Rabbit," they both said, "we want to tell you we are very sorry for our behaviour. We shall never be proud and rude again. We have had our lesson. You saved us from the Weasel, and if ever he comes here again—"

"He won't, he is roasted by now," she interrupted, and told them all her adventures.

"Grey Rabbit," said Squirrel solemnly, shaking her paw for emphasis, "you shall always have the rocking-chair, and sit by the fire. You shall have your breakfast in bed, you shall have toast and coffee."

But Grey Rabbit laughed. "I don't want to lie in bed, I like to work, and I don't want toast and coffee, but I should like to sit in the rocking-chair sometimes, and I should like a party."

So they all lived happily together, and had a fine crop of radishes and carrots, and onions, but no little yellow birds came up.

Sometime I will tell you how Grey Rabbit got her tail back again.

A KISS FOR LITTLE BEAR

Else Holmelund Minarik
Pictures by
Maurice Sendak

"This picture makes me happy,"
said Little Bear.

"Hello, Hen.
This picture is for Grandmother.

Will you take it to her, Hen?"
"Yes, I will," said Hen.

Grandmother was happy.
"This kiss is for Little Bear," she said.

"Will you take it to him, Hen?"
"I will be glad to," said Hen.

Then Hen saw some friends.
She stopped to chat.
"Hello, Frog.
I have a kiss for Little Bear.

It is from his grandmother.
Will you take it to him, Frog?"
"OK," said Frog.

But Frog saw a pond.
He stopped to swim.
"Hey, Cat.
I have a kiss for Little Bear.

It is from his grandmother.
Take it to him, will you?
Cat – hey!
Here I am, in the pond.
Come and get the kiss."

"Oogh!" said Cat.
But he came and got the kiss.

Cat saw a nice spot to sleep.
"Little Skunk,
I have a kiss for Little Bear.

It is from his grandmother.
Take it to him like a good little skunk."

Little Skunk was glad to do that.
But then he saw another little skunk.

She was very pretty.
He gave the kiss to her.

And she gave it back.

And he gave it back.

And then Hen came along.
"Too much kissing," she said.

"But this is Little Bear's kiss,
from his grandmother,"
said Little Skunk.

"Indeed!" said Hen.
"Who has it now?"

Little Skunk had it.
Hen got it back.

She ran to Little Bear,
and she gave him the kiss.

"It is from your grandmother,"
she said.
"It is for the picture you sent her."

"Take one back to her,"
said Little Bear.
"No," said Hen.
"It gets all mixed up!"

The skunks decided to get married.

They had a lovely wedding.

Everyone came.

And Little Bear was best man.

my naughty little sister at the party

dorothy edwards · shirley hughes · my

naughty little sister at the party

dorothy edwards · shirley hughes · my

naughty little sister at the party

dorothy edwards · shirley hughes · my

naughty little sister at the party

dorothy edwards · shirley hughes · my

naughty little sister at the party

dorothy edwards · shirley hughes · my

naughty little sister at the party

dorothy edwards · shirley hughes · my

naughty little sister at the party

My Naughty Little Sister at the Party

Dorothy Edwards & Shirley Hughes

You wouldn't think there could be another child as naughty as my naughty little sister, would you? But there was. There was a thoroughly bad boy who was my naughty little sister's best boy-friend, and this boy's name was Harry.

This Bad Harry and my naughty little sister used to play together quite a lot in Harry's garden, or in our garden, and got up to dreadful mischief between them, picking all the baby gooseberries, and the green blackcurrants, and throwing sand on the flower-beds, and digging up the runner-bean seeds, and all the naughty sorts of things you never, never do in the garden.

Now, one day this Bad Harry's birthday was near, and Bad Harry's mother said he could have a birthday-party and invite lots of children to tea. So Bad Harry came round to our house with a pretty card in an envelope for my naughty little sister, and this card was an invitation asking my naughty little sister to come to the birthday-party.

Bad Harry told my naughty little sister that there would be a lovely tea with jellies and sandwiches and birthday-cake, and my naughty little sister said, "Jolly good."

And every time she thought about the party she said, "Nice tea and birthday-cake." Wasn't she greedy? And when the party day came she didn't make any fuss when my mother dressed her in her new green party-dress, and her green party-shoes and her green hair-ribbon, and she didn't fidget and she didn't wriggle her head about when she was having her hair combed, she kept as still as still, because she was so pleased to think about the party, and when my mother said, "Now, what must you say at the party?" my naughty little sister said, "I must say, 'nice tea'."

But my mother said, "No, no, that *would* be a greedy thing to say. You must say, 'please' and 'thank you' like a good polite child, at tea-time, and say, 'thank you very much for having me', when the party is over."

And my naughty little sister said, "All right, Mother, I promise."

So, my mother took my naughty little sister to the party, and what do you think the silly little girl did as soon as she got there? She went up to Bad Harry's mother and she said very quickly, "Please-and-thank-you, and thank-you-very-much-for-having-me," all at once – just like that, before she forgot to be polite, and then she said, "Now, may I have a lovely tea?"

Wasn't that rude and greedy? But Harry's mother said, "I'm afraid you will have to wait until all the other children are here, but Harry shall show you the tea-table if you like."

Bad Harry looked very smart in a blue party-suit, with white socks and shoes and a real man's haircut, and he said, "Come on, I'll show you."

So they went into the tea-room and there was the birthday-tea spread out on the table. Bad Harry's mother had made red jellies and yellow jellies, and blancmanges and biscuits and sandwiches and cakes-with-cherries-on, and a big birthday-cake with white icing on it and candles and "Happy Birthday Harry" written on it.

My naughty little sister's eyes grew bigger and bigger, and Bad Harry said, "There's something else in the larder. It's going to be a surprise treat, but you shall see it because you are my best girlfriend."

So Bad Harry took my naughty little sister out into the kitchen and they took chairs and climbed up to the larder shelf – which is a dangerous thing to do, and it would have been their own faults if they had fallen down – and Bad Harry showed my naughty little sister a lovely spongy trifle, covered with creamy stuff and with silver balls and jelly-sweets on the top. And my naughty little sister stared more than ever because she liked spongy trifle better than jellies or blancmanges or biscuits or sandwiches or cakes-with-cherries-on, or even birthday-cake, so she said, "For me."

Bad Harry said, "For me too," because he liked spongy trifle best as well.

Then Bad Harry's mother called to them and said, "Come along, the other children are arriving."

So they went to say, "How do you do!" to the other children, and then Bad Harry's mother said, "I think we will have a few games now before tea – just until everyone has arrived."

All the other children stood in a ring and Bad Harry's mother said, "Ring O'Roses first, I think." And all the nice party children said, "Oh, we'd like that."

But my naughty little sister said, "No Ring O'Roses – nasty Ring O'Roses" – just like that, because she didn't like Ring O'Roses very much, and Bad Harry said, "Silly game." So Bad Harry and my naughty little sister stood and watched the others. The other children sang beautifully too, they sang:

"Ring O'Ring O'Roses,
A pocket full of posies –
A-tishoo, a-tishoo, we all fall down."

And they all fell down and laughed, but Harry and my naughty little sister didn't laugh. They got tired of watching and they went for a little walk. Do you know where they went to?

Yes. To the larder. To take another look at the spongy trifle. They climbed up on to the chairs to look at it really properly. It was very pretty.

"Ring O'Ring O'Roses" sang the good party children.

"Nice jelly-sweets," said my naughty little sister. "Nice silver balls," and she looked at that terribly bad Harry and he looked at her.

"Take one," said that naughty boy, and my naughty little sister did take one, she took a red jelly-sweet from the top of the trifle; and then Bad Harry took a green jelly-sweet; and then my naughty little sister took a yellow jelly-sweet and a silver ball, and then Bad Harry took three jelly sweets, red, green and yellow, and six silver balls. One, two, three, four, five, six, and put them all in his mouth at once.

Now some of the creamy stuff had come off on Bad Harry's fingers and he liked it very much, so he put his fingers into the creamy stuff on the trifle, and took some of it off and ate it, and my naughty little sister ate some too. I'm sorry to have to tell you this, because I feel so ashamed of them, and expect you feel ashamed of them too.

I hope you aren't too shocked to hear any more? Because, do you know, those two bad children forgot all about the party and the nice children all singing "Ring O'Roses". They took a spoon each and scraped off the creamy stuff and ate it, and then they began to eat the nice spongy inside.

Bad Harry said, "Now we've made the trifle look so untidy, no one else will want any, so we may as well eat it all up." So they dug away into the spongy inside of the trifle and found lots of nice fruit bits inside. It was a very big trifle, but those greedy children ate and ate.

Then, just as they had nearly finished the whole big trifle, the "Ring O'Roses"-ing stopped, and Bad Harry's mother called, "Where are you two? We are ready for tea."

Then my naughty little sister was very frightened. Because she knew she had been very naughty, and she looked at Bad Harry and *he* knew *he* had been very naughty, and they both felt terrible. Bad Harry had a creamy mess of trifle all over his face, and even in his real man's haircut, and my naughty little sister had made her new green party-dress all trifly – you know how it happens if you eat too quickly and greedily.

"It's tea-time," said Bad Harry, and he looked at my naughty little sister, and my naughty little sister thought of the jellies and the cakes and the sandwiches, and all the other things, and she felt very full of trifle, and she said, "Don't want any."

And do you know what she did? Just as Bad Harry's mother came into the kitchen, my naughty little sister slipped out of the door, and ran and ran all the way home. It was a good thing our home was only down the street and no roads to cross, or I don't know what would have happened to her.

Bad Harry's mother was so cross when she saw the trifle, that she sent Bad Harry straight to bed, and he had to stay there and hear all the nice children enjoying themselves.

I don't know what happened to him in the night, but I know that my naughty little sister wasn't at all a well girl, from having eaten so much trifle – and I also know that she doesn't like spongy trifle any more.

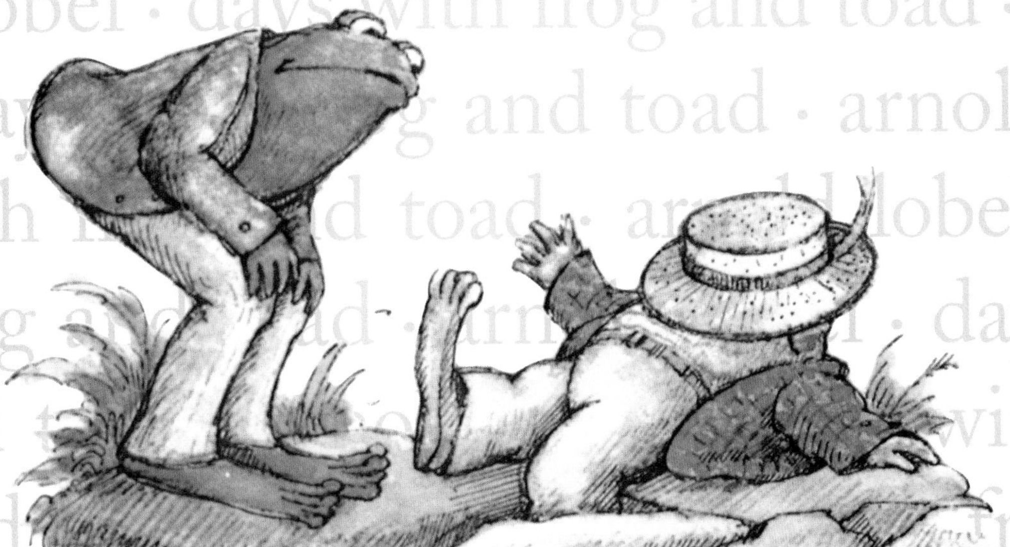

THE
HAT

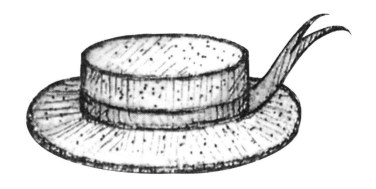

Arnold Lobel

On Toad's birthday
Frog gave him a hat.
Toad was delighted.
"Happy birthday," said Frog.
Toad put on the hat.
It fell down over his eyes.
"I am sorry," said Frog.
"That hat is much too big for you.
I will give you something else."
"No," said Toad. "This hat
is your present to me. I like it.
I will wear it the way it is."

Frog and Toad went for a walk.

Toad tripped over a rock.

He bumped into a tree.

He fell in a hole.

"Frog," said Toad,

"I can't see anything.

I will not be able to wear

your beautiful present.

This is a sad birthday for me."

Frog and Toad
were sad
for a while.
Then Frog said,
"Toad, here is what you must do.
Tonight when you go to bed
you must think
some very big thoughts.
Those big thoughts will make
your head grow larger.
In the morning
your new hat may fit."
"What a good idea," said Toad.

That night when Toad went to bed
he thought the biggest thoughts
that he could think.
Toad thought about
giant sunflowers.
He thought about tall oak trees.
He thought about high mountains
covered with snow.

Then Toad fell asleep.

Frog came into Toad's house.

He came in quietly.

Frog found the hat
and took it to his house.

Frog poured some water on the hat.

He put the hat

in a warm place to dry.

It began to shrink.

That hat grew smaller and smaller.

Frog went back to Toad's house.

Toad was still fast asleep.

Frog put the hat back on the hook
where he found it.

When Toad woke up in the morning,
he put the hat on his head.

It was just the right size.

Toad ran to Frog's house.

"Frog, Frog!" he cried.

"All those big thoughts
have made my head
much larger.

Now I can wear your present!"

Frog and Toad went for a walk.

Toad did not trip
over a rock.

He did not bump into a tree.

He did not fall
in a hole.

It turned out to be
a very pleasant
day after Toad's birthday.

he adventures of toad · kenneth grahame
h shepard · the adventures of toad
enneth grahame · e h shepard · the
dventures of toad · kenneth grahame · e h
hepard · the adventures of toad · kenneth
rahame · e h shepard · the adventures of
oad · kenneth … shepard · the
dventures … rahame · e h
hepard · th … ad · kenneth
rahame · e … dventures of
oad · kenn … shepard · the
dventures … grahame · e h

hepard · the adventures of toad · kenneth
rahame · e h shepard · the adventures of
oad · kenneth grahame · e h shepard · the
dventures of toad · kenneth grahame · e h
hepard · the adventures of toad · kenneth
rahame · e h shepard · the adventures of
oad · kenneth grahame · e h shepard · the
dventures of toad · kenneth grahame · e h

THE
ADVENTURES
OF
TOAD

Kenneth Grahame

ILLUSTRATED BY

E H Shepard

It was a bright morning in the early part of summer. The Mole and the Water Rat had been up since dawn very busy on matters connected with boats and the opening of the boating season; painting and varnishing and mending paddles and so on.

They were finishing breakfast in their little parlour when a heavy knock sounded at the door.

"Bother!" said the Rat, all over egg. "See who it is, Mole, like a good chap."

The Mole went to attend the summons, and the Rat heard him utter a cry of surprise. Then he flung the parlour door open, and announced with much importance, "Mr Badger!"

This was a wonderful thing, indeed, that the Badger should pay a formal call on them, or indeed on anybody.

The Badger strode into the room with an expression full of seriousness.

"The hour has come!" he said with great solemnity.

"What hour?" asked the Rat uneasily, glancing at the clock on the mantelpiece.

"Why, Toad's hour!" replied the Badger. "The hour of Toad! I said I would take him in hand as soon as the winter was well over, and I'm going to take him in hand to-day!"

"Toad's hour, of course!" cried the Mole. "I remember now! *We'll* teach him to be a sensible Toad!"

"This very morning," continued the Badger, "another new and exceptionally powerful motor-car will arrive at Toad Hall. We must be up and doing ere it is too late. You two animals will accompany me instantly to Toad Hall, and the work of rescue shall be accomplished."

"Right you are!" cried the Rat. "We'll convert him! He'll be the most converted Toad that ever was before we've done!"

They set off on their mission of mercy and reached Toad Hall to find a shiny new motor-car in front of the house, and Mr Toad, arrayed in goggles, cap and gaiters, swaggering down the steps.

"Hullo!" he cried cheerfully. "You're just in time to come with me for a jolly – to come – for a – er – jolly –"

His hearty accents faltered as he noticed the stern look on the countenances of his silent friends.

The Badger strode up the steps. "Take him inside," he said sternly to his companions. Toad was hustled through the door, struggling and protesting.

"Now, then!" said Badger, "first of all, take those ridiculous things off!"

"Shan't!" replied Toad.

"Take them off him, then, you two," ordered the Badger briefly.

They had to lay Toad out on the floor, kicking and calling all sorts of names, before they could get his motor-clothes off him.

"You knew it must come to this, sooner or later, Toad," Badger explained. "You're getting us animals a bad name by your furious driving and your smashes and your rows with the police.

Now, I don't want to be too hard on you. I'll make one more effort to bring you to reason. Come with me and hear some facts about yourself."

He took Toad firmly by the arm, led him into a room and closed the door.

"*That's* no good!" said the Rat contemptuously. "*Talking* to Toad'll never cure him. He'll *say* anything."

After some three-quarters of an hour the Badger reappeared, leading by the paw a very limp and dejected Toad.

His skin hung baggily about him, his legs wobbled, and his cheeks were furrowed by the tears so plentifully called forth by the Badger's moving discourse.

"Sit down, Toad," said the Badger kindly. "My friends, I am pleased to inform you that Toad has at last seen the error of his ways and has undertaken to give up motor-cars for ever. Now, Toad, I want you solemnly to repeat, before your friends here, what you admitted to me just now. First, you are sorry for what you've done, and see the folly of it all?"

There was a long, long pause. Toad looked desperately this way and that. At last he spoke.

"No!" he said a little sullenly, but stoutly. "I'm *not* sorry. And it wasn't folly at all! It was simply glorious!"

"What?" cried the Badger, scandalized. "Didn't you tell me just now, in there—"

"O, yes, yes, in *there*," said Toad. "I'd have said anything in *there*. You're so eloquent, dear Badger. But I'm not a bit sorry really. On the contrary, I faithfully promise that the very first motor-car I see, poop-poop! off I go in it!"

"Told you so," observed the Rat.

"Very well," said the Badger firmly. "Since you won't yield to persuasion, we'll try force. Take him upstairs, you two, and lock him up in his bedroom."

"It's for your own good, Toady," said the Rat kindly, as Toad, kicking and struggling, was hauled up the stairs by his two friends. "No more of those incidents with the police," he went on as they thrust him into his bedroom.

They descended the stair, Toad shouting abuse at them through the keyhole.

"I've never seen Toad so determined," said the Badger, sighing. "However, we will see it out. He must never be left an instant unguarded."

They arranged watches accordingly, and strove to divert Toad's mind into fresh channels. But his interest in other matters did not seem to revive, and he grew apparently languid and depressed.

One morning the Rat, whose turn it was to go on duty, went upstairs to relieve Badger. "Toad's in bed," said Badger. "Can't get much out of him, so look out! When Toad's quiet and submissive, he's at his artfullest. Well, I must be off."

"How are you to-day, old chap?" inquired the Rat cheerfully, as he approached Toad's bedside.

"Mole is out with Badger, so I'll do my best to amuse you. Now jump up, there's a good fellow!"

"Dear, kind Rat," murmured Toad. "How little you realize my condition, and how very far I am from 'jumping up' now – if ever. But do not trouble about me. I'm a nuisance, I know."

"You are, indeed," said the Rat. "But I'd take any trouble on earth for you, if only you'd be a sensible animal."

"Then, Ratty," murmured Toad, more feebly than ever, "I beg you – for the last time, probably – to step round to the village as quickly as possible – even now it may be too late – and fetch the doctor. And, while you are about it – would you ask the lawyer to step up?"

"O, he must be really bad!" the Rat said to himself as he hurried from the room, locking the door behind him. "I've known Toad fancy himself bad before, but I've never heard him ask for a lawyer!" He ran off on his errand of mercy.

Toad hopped lightly out of bed as soon as he heard the key turn in the lock. Then, laughing heartily, he dressed quickly and, knotting the

sheets from his bed together and tying one end round the window, he slid to the ground and marched off whistling a merry tune.

It was a gloomy luncheon for Rat when Badger and Mole returned and he had to face them at table with his pitiful story.

Meanwhile, Toad was walking briskly along, some miles from home. "Smart work that!" he remarked to himself, chuckling. "Poor old Ratty! A worthy fellow, but very little intelligence. I must take him in hand some day."

He strode along till he reached a little town, where the sign of "The Red Lion" reminded him that he was exceedingly hungry. He marched into the inn and sat down to eat.

He was about half-way through his meal when a familiar sound made him fall a-trembling all over. The poop-poop! drew nearer, the car could be heard to turn into the inn-yard, and Toad had to hold on to the leg of the table to conceal his overmastering emotion.

Presently, the party entered the room, hungry and talkative. Toad listened for a time. At last he could stand it no longer. He paid his bill and sauntered round quietly to the inn-yard. "There cannot be any harm," he said to himself, "in my only just *looking* at it!"

The car stood in the middle of the yard, quite unattended. Toad walked slowly round it, musing deeply.

"I wonder," he said to himself, "if this sort of car *starts* easily?"

Next moment, hardly knowing how it came about, he had hold of the handle and was turning it. As the familiar sound broke forth, the old passion seized on Toad and completely mastered him, body and soul. As if in a dream he found himself, somehow, seated in the driver's seat. He swung the car out through the archway, increased his pace and, as the car leapt forth on the high road, he was only conscious that he was once more Toad at his best and highest, Toad the terror, the Lord of the lone trail!

"This ruffian," said the Chairman of the Bench of Magistrates, "has been found guilty of stealing a valuable motor-car, driving to the public danger, and gross impertinence to the police.

"Mr Clerk, what is the very stiffest penalty we can impose for each of these offences?"

The Clerk scratched his nose. "Some people would consider," he observed, "that stealing the motor-car was the worst offence; and so it is. But cheeking the police undoubtedly carries the severest penalty; and so it ought. Supposing you were to say twelve months for the theft; three

years for the furious driving, and fifteen years for the cheek, which was pretty bad sort of cheek, judging by what we've heard, those figures, added together, tot up to nineteen years! Better make it a round twenty and be on the safe side."

"Excellent!" said the Chairman.

Then the brutal minions of the law fell upon the hapless Toad.

They loaded him with chains, and dragged him from the Court House, shrieking, praying, protesting; across the market-place, below the portcullis of the grim old castle, on and on, till they reached the dungeon that lay in the innermost keep. The rusty key creaked in the lock, the great door clanged behind them; and Toad was a helpless prisoner in the remotest dungeon of the best-guarded keep of the stoutest castle in all of England.

Toad flung himself on the floor, and abandoned himself to dark despair. "This is the end of everything," he said, "the end of the career of the popular and handsome Toad, the Toad so free and careless and debonair! Stupid animal that I was! O wise old Badger! O intelligent Rat and sensible Mole! O unhappy and forsaken Toad!" With lamentations such as these he passed his days and nights for several weeks.

Now the gaoler had a daughter who was particularly fond of animals. This kind-hearted girl, pitying the misery of Toad, said to her father one day, "Father! I can't bear to see that poor beast so unhappy and getting so thin! Let me have the managing of him!"

Her father replied that she could do what she liked with him. He was tired of Toad and his sulks and his airs.

So that day she knocked at the door of Toad's cell.

"Cheer up, Toad," she said coaxingly. "And do try and eat a bit of dinner. I've brought you some of mine!"

But still Toad wailed and kicked with his legs, and refused to be comforted. So the wise girl retired for the time.

When she returned, some hours later, she carried a tray with a plate piled up with very hot buttered toast. The smell of that buttered toast simply talked to Toad; talked of warm kitchens, of breakfasts on frosty mornings and cosy parlour firesides on winter evenings.

Toad sat up, dried his eyes, munched his toast and soon began talking about himself and how important he was, and what a lot his friends thought of him.

The gaoler's daughter saw that the topic was doing him good and encouraged him to go on. When she said good night, Toad was very much the same self-satisfied animal that he had been of old.

They had many talks together after that and the girl grew very sorry for Toad.

One morning the girl was very thoughtful.

"Toad," she said presently, "I have an aunt who is a washerwoman."

"There, there," said Toad affably, "never mind; *I* have several aunts who *ought* to be washerwomen."

"Do be quiet, Toad," said the girl. "You talk too much. As I said, I have an aunt who is a washerwoman. Now, you're very rich, and she's very poor. A few pounds wouldn't make any difference to you, and it would mean a lot to her. Now, I think if she were properly approached, she would let you have her dress and bonnet and so on, and you could escape as the official washerwoman. You're very alike – particularly about the figure."

"We're *not*," said the Toad in a huff. "I have a very elegant figure – for what I am. And you wouldn't surely have Mr Toad of Toad Hall going about the country disguised as a washerwoman?"

"Then you can stop here as a Toad," replied the girl with much spirit.

Toad was always ready to admit himself in the wrong. "You are a good, clever girl," he said. "Introduce me to your worthy aunt, if you will be so kind."

Next evening the girl ushered her aunt into Toad's cell. In return for his cash, Toad received a cotton print gown, an apron, a shawl and a rusty black bonnet.

Shaking with laughter, the girl proceeded to "hook-and-eye" him into the gown, and tied the strings of the bonnet under his chin. "You're the very image of her," she giggled.

With a quaking heart, Toad set forth. But he was soon agreeably surprised to find how easy everything was. The washerwoman's squat figure seemed a passport for every barred door and grim gateway. The humorous sallies to which he was subjected formed his chief danger; for Toad was an animal with a strong sense of his own dignity.

He kept his temper, however, though with difficulty.

It seemed hours before he crossed the last courtyard and dodged the outspread arms of the last warder, pleading with simulated passion for just one farewell embrace. But at last he was free!

He walked quickly towards the lights of the town, not knowing what he should do next.

As he walked along, his attention was caught by some red and green lights.

"Aha!" he thought, "this is a piece of luck! A railway-station."

He made his way to the station and went to buy his ticket. He mechanically put his fingers where his waistcoat pocket should have been. But he found – not only no money, but no pocket to hold it!

To his horror he recollected that he had left both coat and waistcoat in his cell, and with them his money, keys, watch – all that makes life worth living.

Full of despair, he wandered blindly down the platform where the train was standing and tears trickled down his nose. Very soon his escape would be discovered and he would be caught and dragged back to prison. What was to be done? As he pondered, he found himself opposite the engine, which was being oiled by its affectionate driver.

"Hullo, mother!" said the engine-driver, "what's the trouble?"

"O, sir!" said Toad, crying, "I am a poor washerwoman, and I've lost all my money, and can't pay for a ticket, and I *must* get home to-night. O dear, O dear!"

"Well, I'll tell you what I'll do," said the good engine-driver.

"If you'll wash a few shirts for me when you get home and send 'em along, I'll give you a ride on my engine."

The Toad's misery turned into rapture as he eagerly scrambled up into the cab of the engine.

Of course, he had never washed a shirt in his life, and couldn't if he tried; but he thought: "When I get home and have money again, I will send the engine-driver enough to pay for quite a quantity of washing."

The guard waved his flag, and the train moved out of the station.

Toad began to skip up and down and shout and sing, to the great astonishment of the engine-driver, who had come across washer-women before, but never one at all like this.

They had covered many a mile, and Toad was considering what he would have for supper as soon as he got home, when the engine-driver, with a puzzled expression on his face, said: "It's very strange, we're the last train running in this direction to-night, yet I could be sworn that I heard another following us!"

Toad ceased his frivolous antics at once. He became grave and depressed.

Presently the driver called out, "I can see it clearly now! It is an engine on our rails, coming along at a great pace! It looks as if we were being pursued! They are gaining on us fast! And the engine is crowded with policemen, waving truncheons and all shouting 'Stop, stop! stop!'"

Then Toad fell on his knees and cried, "Save me, kind Mr Engine-driver! I am not the simple washerwoman I seem! I am the well-known and popular Mr Toad, and I have just escaped from a dungeon into which my enemies had flung me! I only borrowed a motor-car while the owners were at lunch. I didn't mean to steal it; but magistrates take such harsh views of high-spirited actions."

The engine-driver looked very grave.

"I fear that you have been indeed a wicked toad," he said, "and I ought to give you up to justice. But the sight of an animal in tears always makes me feel soft-hearted. So cheer up, Toad! I'll do my best and we may beat them yet!"

They piled on more coals; the furnace roared, the sparks flew, the engine leapt and swung, but still their pursuers slowly gained.

The engine-driver wiped his brow and said, "I'm afraid it's no good, Toad. You see, they have the better engine. There's only one thing left for

us to do, and it's your only chance, so attend very carefully to what I tell you. A short way ahead of us is a long tunnel, and on the other side of that the line passes through a thick wood. Now, I will put on all the speed I can while we are running through the tunnel.

"When we are through, I will put on brakes as hard as I can, and the moment it's safe to do so you must jump and hide in the wood, before they get through the tunnel and see you. Then I will go full speed ahead again, and they can chase *me* for as long as they like. Now, be ready to jump when I tell you!"

They piled on more coals and the train shot into the tunnel. They shot out at the other end into fresh air and the peaceful moonlight, and saw the wood lying dark and helpful upon either side of the line. The driver put on brakes, and as the train slowed down to almost a walking pace he called out, "Now, jump!"

Toad jumped, rolled down a short embankment, picked himself up unhurt, scrambled into the wood and hid.

Peeping out, he saw his train get up speed again and disappear.

Then out of the tunnel burst the pursuing engine, roaring and whistling, her motley crew waving their weapons and shouting, "Stop! stop!" When they were past, Toad had a hearty laugh.

But he soon stopped laughing when he came to consider that it was now very late and dark and cold, and he was in an unknown wood, with no money and no chance of supper and still far from home. He dared not leave the shelter of the trees, so he struck into the wood, leaving the railway far behind him. He found the wood strange and unfriendly.

An owl, swooping noiselessly, brushed his shoulder, making him jump. A fox looked at him sarcastically and said, "Hullo, washerwoman! Half a pair of socks short this week! Mind it doesn't occur again!" and swaggered off, sniggering. Toad looked for a stone to throw at him, but could not find one.

At last, cold, hungry, and tired out, he sought the shelter of a hollow tree, made himself as comfortable a bed as he could, and slept soundly till morning.

The next morning, Toad was called early by bright sunlight streaming in on him. Sitting up, he rubbed his eyes and wondered for a moment where he was; then he remembered – he was free!

Free! He was warm from end to end as he thought of the jolly world outside, waiting eagerly for him to make his triumphal entrance, anxious to help him and to keep him company, as it always had been in days of old before misfortune fell upon him. He shook himself, combed the dry leaves out of his hair with his fingers and marched forth into the comfortable morning sun.

homas the tank engine · the rev w
wdry · thomas the tank engine · the rev
v awdry · thomas the tank engine · the
ev w awdry · thomas the tank engine
he rev w awdry · thomas the tank
ngine · the rev w awdry · thomas the
ank engine · the rev w awdry · thomas
he tank engin w awdry
homas the t he rev w
wdry · thomas gine · the rev
v awdry · tank engine · the

ev w awdry · thomas the tank engine
he rev w awdry · thomas the tank
ngine · the rev w awdry · thomas the
ank engine · the rev w awdry · thomas
he tank engine · the rev w awdry
homas the tank engine · the rev w
wdry · thomas the tank engine · the rev

Thomas

and

Gordon

The Rev W Awdry

THOMAS was a tank engine who lived at a Big Station. He had six small wheels, a short stumpy funnel, a short stumpy boiler, and a short stumpy dome.

He was a fussy little engine, always pulling coaches about. He pulled them to the station ready for the big engines to take out on long journeys; and when trains came in, and the people had got out, he would pull the empty coaches away, so that the big engines could go and rest.

He was a cheeky little engine, too. He thought no engine worked as hard as he did. So he used to play tricks on them. He liked best of all to come quietly beside a big engine dozing on a siding and make him jump.

"Peep, peep, peep, pip, peep! Wake up, lazybones!" he would whistle, "why don't you work hard like me?"

Then he would laugh rudely and run away to find some more coaches.

One day Gordon was resting on a siding. He was very tired. The big Express he always pulled had been late, and he had had to run as fast as he could to make up for lost time.

He was just going to sleep when Thomas came up in his cheeky way.

"Wake up, lazybones," he whistled, "do some hard work for a change – you can't catch me!" and he ran off laughing.

Instead of going to sleep again, Gordon thought how he could pay Thomas out.

One morning Thomas wouldn't wake up. His Driver and Fireman couldn't make him start. His fire went out and there was not enough steam.

It was nearly time for the Express. The people were waiting, but the coaches weren't ready.

At last Thomas started. "Oh, dear! Oh, dear!" he yawned.

"Come on," said the coaches. "Hurry up."

Thomas gave them a rude bump, and started for the station.

"Don't stop dawdling, don't stop dawdling," he grumbled.

"Where have you been? Where have you been?" asked the coaches crossly.

Thomas fussed into the station where Gordon was waiting.

"Poop, poop. Hurry up, you," said Gordon crossly.

"Peep, pip, peep. Hurry yourself," said cheeky Thomas.

"Yes," said Gordon, "I will," and almost before the coaches had stopped moving Gordon came out of his siding and was coupled to the train.

"Poop, poop," he whistled. "Get in quickly, please." So the people got in quickly, the signal went down, the clock struck the hour, the guard waved his green flag, and Gordon was ready to start.

Thomas usually pushed behind the big trains to help them start. But he was always uncoupled first, so that when the train was running nicely he could stop and go back.

This time he was late, and Gordon started so quickly that they forgot to uncouple Thomas.

"Poop, poop," said Gordon.

"Peep, peep, peep," whistled Thomas.

"Come on! Come on!" puffed Gordon to the coaches.

"Pull harder! Pull harder!" puffed Thomas to Gordon.

The heavy train slowly began to move out of the station.

The train went faster and faster; too fast for Thomas. He wanted to stop but he couldn't.

"Peep! Peep! Stop! Stop!" he whistled.

"Hurry, hurry, hurry," laughed Gordon in front.

"You can't get away. You can't get away," laughed the coaches.

Poor Thomas was going faster than he had ever gone before. He was out of breath and his wheels hurt him, but he had to go on.

"I shall never be the same again," he thought sadly. "My wheels will be quite worn out."

At last they stopped at a station. Everyone laughed to see Thomas puffing and panting behind.

They uncoupled him, put him on to a turntable and then he ran on a siding out of the way.

"Well, little Thomas," chuckled Gordon as he passed, "now you know what hard work means, don't you?"

Poor Thomas couldn't answer, he had no breath. He just puffed slowly away to rest, and had a long, long drink.

He went home very slowly, and was careful afterwards never to be cheeky to Gordon again.

The Childhood Collection
first published in Great Britain 1998
by Heinemann Young Books
an imprint of Egmont Children's Books Limited
Michelin House, 81 Fulham Road, London SW3 6RB

ISBN 0 434 80389 8
10 9 8 7 6 5 4 3 2 1

A CIP catalogue record for this book is available
from the British Library

Printed in Spain

Editor: Alison Ritchie
Art Director: Genevieve Webster

the three little wolves and the big bad pig
at pooh corner for eeyore the story of ba
rabbit my naughty little sister at the part
engine the adventures of toad a kiss for l
bad pig cops and robbers in which a hous
of babar the squirrel the hare and the litt
party days with frog and toad thomas th
for little bear the three little wolves and t
house is built at pooh corner for eeyore
the little grey rabbit my naughty little s
thomas the tank engine the adventures
wolves and the big bad pig cops and robb
for eeyore the story of babar the squir
naughty little sister at the party days with
adventures of toad a kiss for little bear the
and robbers in which a house is built at p
squirrel the hare and the little grey rabb
with frog and toad thomas the tank engin